JAMES STEVENSON

What's Under My Bed ?

MULBERRY BOOKS New York

First Mulberry Edition, 1990
10 9 8 7 6 5 4 3 2 1

Library of Congress Cataloging in Publication Data

Stevenson, James [date]
What's under my bed?
Summary: Grandpa tells his two young houseguests
a story about his own childhood when he was
scared at bedtime.
[1. Bedtime—Fiction. 2. Grandfathers—Fiction.
3. Fear—Fiction] I. Title.
PZ7.S84748Wh 1983 [E] 83-1454
ISBN 0-688-09350-7

"Time for bed," said Grandpa. "I hope
that story wasn't too scary for you."
"Oh, no," said Mary Ann.
"Not for us," said Louie.

"Sleep well," said Grandpa.

"Would you leave the door open a little?" said Mary Ann.

"Or a lot?" said Louie.

"Certainly," said Grandpa. "Good night."

"I didn't believe that story, did you?" said Mary Ann.
"Of course not," said Louie. "Especially the monster part."
"And the screaming part," said Mary Ann.

"Do you hear something?" asked Mary Ann, a few minutes later.
"Like what?" said Louie.
"Like something coming up the stairs," said Mary Ann.
"It's nothing," said Louie.

"Look at that shadow on the wall,"
said Mary Ann. "Here it comes."

"It's getting bigger," said Louie.
The door opened wide.

It was only Leonard, wagging his tail.

For a while it was quiet.
Then Mary Ann said,
"I think there's something
under my bed."

"There's nothing under your bed,"
said Louie.
"How do you know?"
said Mary Ann.

"I just know," said Louie.
"Take a look," said Mary Ann.
"I'm too tired," said Louie.

"I bet you're afraid to put your feet
over the edge," said Mary Ann.
"No, I'm not," said Louie.
He started to get out of bed.

Louie stepped on Leonard.
Leonard jumped and howled.
Mary Ann yelled.

Then they all ran downstairs.

"Well, hello," said Grandpa. "What seems to be the trouble?"
"Something was under our beds," said Mary Ann.
"Is that so?" said Grandpa.
"Why, the very same thing happened to me once.

It was long ago, when I was visiting my grandparents.
I was about your age. The house was strange.
I was a little bit scared on my way to bed.

As I went up the stairs, glittery eyes stared at me through the window…''

''Those were probably just fireflies, Grandpa,'' said Louie.
''Perhaps you're right,'' said Grandpa.

"My room was at the end of a long, long hall.

I went into my room, put on my pajamas,

picked up a book and read for a while.

Suddenly, I realized I had
forgotten to look under
the bed. I worked up my
nerve and took a peek.

It was awful! A creature
with wild hair, no head, and a long tail
was standing there.''

"But, Grandpa," said Mary Ann,
"wasn't that your shoes and your
bathrobe and your hairbrush,
just where you had left them?"
"Why, that's *just* what it was,"
said Grandpa.

"I got back into bed.

Then I heard some horrible sounds...little creatures on stilts.
They went *Gnik gnok*."

"Grandpa, was there a big grandfather
clock in the hall?" said Mary Ann.
"Why, yes, there was," said Grandpa.
"What did it sound like?" said
Mary Ann.
"Oh," said Grandpa. "I see what
you mean.

"Probably not a big bird,
Grandpa," said Louie.
"No?" said Grandpa. "Then
what could it have been?"
"A few moths," said Louie.

I closed my eyes. A huge and terrible bird
flew in. I could feel its feathers on my face."

"Just what it was,"
said Grandpa.

"Probably some cats jumping on garbage cans," said Mary Ann. "Probably," said Grandpa.

"But then, outside my window I heard pirates fighting with swords...*clash, clash!*"

"Then the bats came in. I could hear them fluttering all around me."

"Wait," said Louie.
"Yes?" said Grandpa.
"Could it have been the wind fluttering the pages of your book?" said Louie.
"Not only could have been," said Grandpa. "It was."

"You should have closed the window," said Mary Ann.
"Just what I did," said Grandpa.
"All quiet after that?" asked Louie.
"Yes," said Grandpa.

"You should have shut the
window tighter," said Mary Ann.
"Right you are!" said Grandpa.
"I got up and shut the window
tighter."

"Until the ghosts started wailing and moaning."

"Safe at last, eh?" said Louie.
"I *thought* so," said Grandpa.

"But then I heard the skeletons climbing up the side of the house. Their bones were creaking as they climbed."

"Were you scared, Grandpa?" said Mary Ann.
"Indeed I was," said Grandpa.
"You shouldn't have been," said Mary Ann. "It was the branches of the tree, creaking in the wind."
"How did you know?" said Grandpa.

"Well, it was getting hot so I foolishly opened the window again."

"Not a good idea?" said Louie.
"No," said Grandpa. "The light blew out."
"Were you scared in the dark, Grandpa?" said Mary Ann.
"Just until I got used to it," said Grandpa.
"Then you felt better?" said Louie.

"No, worse," said Grandpa. "Then I could see
what was coming in the window."
"Such as?" said Mary Ann.
"Oh," said Grandpa,

"goblins, witches, spiders, giants,
monsters, dragons, slitherers, and creepers,
leeches that wriggled, wretches that giggled,

peaches that screeched, creatures that reached and
pinched and poked, nibbled and dribbled,
snapped and stomped and squished,

scratchers and catchers, growlers and howlers,
things that were smelly, or shaky like jelly!

Suddenly, they all started chasing *me*!
I ran out the door.

I could hear something coming after me.
I ran from one room to another, and down the halls.

I ran upstairs and down. Finally,

I stopped to rest.
I looked behind me.
Nothing was there."

"Why it was only my grandpa and grandma.

They thought
maybe I was hungry.

They gave me a big bowl of strawberry ice cream.
I felt much better."